America is Broken

Time 2 MANning Up Series

America is Broken

**Author
Jasper "Mr. Horse" Manning**

ReadersMagnet, LLC

America is Broken: Time 2 MANning Up Series
Copyright © 2021 by Jasper "Mr. Horse" Manning

Published in the United States of America
ISBN Paperback: 978-1-955603-04-1
ISBN eBook: 978-1-955603-03-4

All rights reserved. No part of this publication may be reproduced, stored in a retrieval system or transmitted in any way by any means, electronic, mechanical, photocopy, recording or otherwise without the prior permission of the author except as provided by USA copyright law.

All Bible citations are from the King James Version.

The opinions expressed by the author are not necessarily those of ReadersMagnet, LLC.

ReadersMagnet, LLC
10620 Treena Street, Suite 230 | San Diego, California, 92131 USA
1.619.354.2643 | www.readersmagnet.com

Book design copyright © 2021 by ReadersMagnet, LLC. All rights reserved.
Cover design by Kent Gabutin
Interior design by Renalie Malinao

Contents

Acknowledgement xi
Introduction xiii

Chapter 1 Do Writes Ethics 1
America Is Broken 2
Broken Tears. 4
Things I Miss 6
Children with Cancer 8
The Rock 10
Life's Most Powerful Word. 12
Behind that Smile. 14
Once Upon a Time 15
The Child Support Files. 17
The Biggest Bully 19
Terrioristic Motives. 20
Just Another Black Man 21
Proud to be BLACK. 23
Kool-Aid Fix 25
The Pain of Being Black. 26
Inside A Childs Eyes. 28
Too Much to Ask 30

Heart of a Fighter 31
Black in America 33

Chapter 2   Marriage Do Writes 35
Married and Proud of It 36
The Heart of a Marriage. 37
The Strength of a Man 38
Love in a Woman's Heart 39
The Wife Queen 40
Working Marriage 41
Today I thought about you 43
Snooze Control 44
That Moment 46
The Other Side of Marriage 48
Unfamiliar Presence 50
The Relationship Monster 51
The Dream of Us 53
A Husband's Gratitude 55
Close to each Other 57
Warrior Wife 58
What I Want 60
Greatness 62
Girlfriend and Boyfriend 64
Today I touched an Angel 65
Thought for the Day 66

Chapter 3   Parental Do Writes 67
Grown Little Child 68
Larger Than Life 70
A Mother's Protection 72
Mother's Day 73
Rain on a Sunny Day 75

Tears of the 324th 78
The Game that Never-Ends 80
Mack Earl Tippens 82
Grow Up Young Man 84
The Proud Parent 86
Full Time Mom 88
The Critical Leader 90
Christmas 2020 92
A Manner of Fact 94
As Your Father 95
The Same 97
Teach them to know! 100
Will They Hear You 101

Chapter 4   Do Writes as a Man 103
The Gentleman Thing 104
Lifelong Lesson's 106
The Wants and Needs of a Child 107
Hopes and Dreams. 109
To a Certain Degree 111
The E in Me 113
When I Stand 114
The Honor in Commitment 116
Childhood to Manhood 117
What Do You Expect? 118
The Three Hads 119
The Other Side of Heart's. 121
Afraid to Love. 123
Control 125
Father Figure 127
A Man is as a Man Does. 129

Loving a woman, the right way
Loving a man, the right way 130
The Face of Death 131
The Road to Life 132
Tomorrow "n" Today. 134

Chapter 5   Do Writes Just Because 135
Funny thing the heart. 136
Hear to Ear. 138
Lay Her Down to Sleep 139
Softball with a Soul 140
Make it Work 141
The Land of Math 142
The C in Me. 144
The Power of a Song. 146
That Final Feel Good 148
Selfish until Death 150
I used to be that guy. 152
People are just People 154
He Looks Like Me 155
Success in Failure 157
The Best You Have to Give. 158
Inside a Black Man 160
Somnolence. 162
RAF Alconbury Spartans 164
Things I Can't unsee. 165
Little Stinker 167
Personal Journey 169
The Wrong Team 170

Chapter 6   Christian Do Writes. 173
A Prayer for the Living 175

A Creation Gone Bad 177
Just the facts 179
The Days God Made 181
I Spent the Day with God. 183
The Luxury of Obedience. 185
God is Good. 186
That Question 188
Listening to God 190
The Proud Christian. 191
Wanting and Waiting 192
The Day in a Glance 193
Tears of Angles 194
Peaceful Surroundings 195
The Privilege of Waking up 196
A Passion for Christ 198
Well Hidden. 199
He did not have to But he did anyway. 200
Counting Time. 201
Who am I to die? 203
Giving Thanks to God 205

Index. 213

Acknowledgement

I would like to thank God for watching over me for the past 61 years of my life, and has brought me to the point in my life so that I can share some of the blessings that he has blessed my family and I with. Especially those who have paved the way for me to have this opportunity. Secondly, I would also like to pay homage to our Lord and savior Jesus Christ. I would like to thank the citizens of the United States of America who inspire me daily to express my thoughts and ideas in the form of poetry. The passion, humor, and the appreciation for my own personal journey with my wife mother, father, sisters, and brother's, sons, and daughters, along with other family members.

America is Broken is the second book in this series (Time 2 MANning Up), and is inspired by the first book and all the people who made an impact on my life growing up and has been noted in the 1st book. Enjoy the poems, examine your emotions, and I hope you find it in your heart to have those difficult discussions about the fabric of the United States of America.

Introduction

Someone once said, "Find your purpose in life and then do something about it" This is my WHY?

Our society is blessed and plaque with the various facets of Democracy. In America you have the right to be whatever you want to be if you are willing to work hard for it. This America that we live in, the land of the free for some but not all will continue to be a controversial endeavor. Black Lives Matter really became visible during May 2020 after the murder of George Floyd by Minnesota Police Officers. This murder that was viewed by the entire world on social media revealed the dirty laundry of the American Dream around the world. Our forefathers fought and died for the civil liberties that all Americans enjoy today. As a former member of the United States Air Force. We all have a right to speak out against what is right and wrong, to vote and protest peacefully for a better life. Then the laws of the land will prevail to ensure that our civil liberties which are the foundations of God's Ten Commandments will serve and protect all American citizens.

I proudly served my country so that all Americans can enjoy the civil liberties of life liberty and the pursuit of happiness.

Vocabulary

WEARL – Life through the eyes of Earl Manning based on the way he was raised by parents, aunties, uncles, grandparents, and lessons learned from friends and life's experiences.

Twin Year 2020

Some survived 20/20
While others had to move on
Held Captive by a presidential ego.
This man who governed all alone.

Corona was a virus.
That COVIDED the Wearl
It is why I share these poems.
It did not just affect Earl.

George Floyd showed the Wearl.
The fabric of America's creed
So, the U.S. voted for decency.
It is what our 2021 needs.

We have 19 reasons.
To change the way, we live
In hopes we find an appreciation
For the gifts God continues to give

Judgement day is coming.
For some it has already arrived
Life liberty and the pursuit of happiness
Will the real AMERICA stay alive.

Chapter 1

Do Writes Ethics

America Is Broken

American is broken.
Cracking at the seems
We must destroy RACISM.
Destroying the American Dream

Shot for no reason.
Because of our skin
Since it goes unpunished
It happens again, again and again.

Kneeling on a man's neck
Until he cannot breathe
Condemning America for its anger
We will never concede.

You want us to respect you.
When respect means nothing at all
You continue to knock us down.
Even though stand back up, TALL.

You want the pandemic to end.
So, things go back to what there were.
I hate to inform you, but that will not do.
Change is what we prefer.

Life liberty the pursuit of happiness
A citizen's constitutional rights
If we do not receive equality
We will continue to protest and fight.

What are you afraid of?
That all will be treated the same
For you to be treated like blacks
Now that would be a shame.

Broken Tears

The tears of a woman
They roll and they fall.
The look on her face
Will never tell it all

As the pain runs deep
The heart switch is broken
To love or not to love
Questionable words unspoken

Still the road to happiness
Is very seldom traveled
The slightest glimpse of history
The face becomes unraveled

Life still goes on
And eyes must find its rest
Yes find a way to sleep
But the sleep is not your best

You hold it down when all around
Friends have found their peace
When in your mine you find
Emotions that fail to release

A tear will cry from the drop of an eye
And not know where to fall
You reminisce time you missed
A chance to speak and spill it all.

As tears find the years
To heal that heart in ache
The tears find a way to hide.
For everyone else's sake

Things I Miss

I miss my mom a lot.
By the way and most of all
There were days I would pick up the phone.
And she had already called.

I miss playing football in the streets.
Going out for the long pass
When mom was finally called home
I realize that nothing good lasts.

I miss the country Bar B que's
That used to last all day.
While laughing and drinking soda pops
And we would run and play.

I miss my son when he grew up.
And went about a man's way.
To start his family just like me
And that is why at night I pray.

I miss working out sometimes.
And it is when my body aches.
I would miss the sun if it did not shine.
Because with God's touch we away

I met a woman and fell in love.
And now she loves me back.
I have the love I have always wanted.
And I just do not know how to act.

There are things in this world I miss.
But I never would go back.
And if my wife would stop loving me
Then I would miss her and that is a fact

So, we made an agreement.
To exchange rings and hold hands.
If she would promise to be my woman
Then I would be her man

Children with Cancer

When children suffer
Hearts seem to fall.
God is watching.
We know that is not all.

A child stricken with cancer.
Kimmo's on the way
We all know as adults.
Life is precious every day.

A child must go through.
What we see all the time
If you are not thankful for life
Know I am thankful for mine

The gift to be empathetic.
What children must go through?
Because when a child suffers
It could have been me or you.

When they stand strong
Without knowing how to live
When we as adults live our lives
Still find it hard to give.

So, offer a kind word.
To come from a gentle heart
Because God gave us life
That he did not have to start

So, when children stand strong.
Each day just one more time
I do not know about you.
I give thanks for this life of mine.

The Rock

I lost a friend to a heart attack.
Bowling was his game.
Confident in his ability to bowl.
Rock was his name.

33 years later and a heart attack
God called him home.
He left a wife and two children.
Now they are all alone.

Every time you would see the Rock.
His son was by his side.
He would watch his dad bowl.
And on the floor, he would slide.

He was always trying to find a game.
He was good at what he did.
Even though he was a grown man.
Bowling made him a kid.

He loved to laugh cracking jokes.
One reason bowling was fun.
We all just seem to fit right in
And now his days are done.

People loved to be around him.
And watch him as he would strike.
This is what he loved to do.
This is what he liked.

He will be missed.
Bowling, the ball, and the lane
God has a way of delivering messages.
In this message Rock was his name

RIP
Rock

Life's Most Powerful Word

I should have gone to bed last night.
But I chose to stay awake.
Now my eyes refuse to rise.
But it was my choice to make.

I knew that friend was trouble.
But it was my choice to take.
This just in, he was not my friend.
But it was my choice to make.

I should have paid my rent.
But I had a groove to shake.
Now there is no bed to lay my head.
But it was my choice to make.

I did not listen to my parents.
It is my life for goodness sake.
I heard a song when things go wrong.
But it was my choice to make.

I chose to do the popular
The right thing just seemed fake.
The bible will head whatever is said.
But it was my choice to make.

I knew my instincts were correct.
But my ego was wide awake.
If it does not seem right day or night
You have a choice to make?

When health tells you one thing
Your foot will not find the brake.
Take care of yourself or else.
You will not have a choice to make.

Behind that Smile

We tend to judge the person.
Standing in behind the smile
But if you give them an opportunity
They will show you them after a while.

A smile can only last so long
Before the truth comes out
Depending on what they show you.
You will know what the smile is about.

Some may smile to keep from crying.
Enduring life's ups and downs
If they did not have a reason to smile
They may have a reason to drown.

There may be times you will find.
They are smiling whenever you are around.
This should be a good thing.
You are the reason there is no frown.

Things happen in their lives.
That would put leaves on a naked tree.
By God's grace they stand straight
Because they would bend at the knee

People will tend to gravitate.
To the person behind the smile
So, if that gravity brought them to you
Would it be worth their while?

Once Upon a Time

I am reminded of a simpler time.
With all this time to think
Our government stands on trial.
This whole corona virus thing stinks

A man made virous C.O.V.I.D.-19.
Doing what it is supposed to.
Exposing to you the unexposed
To see who is really the who.

Did you happen to ever wake up?
From a long, long time ago
To see how men treated men.
So that now you are in the know.

It was not pretty, way back then.
And it is certainly, not now.
But it happened, so live with it.
Vote for change, that is the how.

My childhood was somewhat simple.
These worries did not have the time.
To come between my bunny rabbit syrup
Now the bunny in my syrup is blind.

Waking up early in the morning
The nose had a mind of its own.
Compliments of breakfast is ready.
Flap jacks is what we put on.

Shelter in place was on our face.
So, a certain virus would not spread.
You can either listen or eat breakfast.
So that you are either be fed or dead

God has the final say.
With the whole world in his hand
Virus or not it is what we got.
Decisions will determine who stands.

The Child Support Files

Another broken relationship
Another mad mom again
If the man will not what she wants
Then he cannot be a man

A child who is led to believe.
That their dad is a dead beat
While dad is trying to sit down
Mom will not let him have a seat.

Trying to get all she can.
Just because he is the man.
Since he will not bow to her
Then she will not let him stand

Child support is not a problem.
So, when can I see my kid?
Do not make the child suffer.
Because of something we did

You will not answer the cell phone.
While trying to hide my child
Your dad did not want to see you.
Hiding behind a fake smile

Some dads make better moms.
They must and will hit that grind.
Something a young man should see.
A provider is engraved in his mind.

And little girls need their dad.
To avoid those little boys
To be treated the way a dad would
So, they are not used like toys.

Why should the child suffer?
With a life filled with regret
Led to believe dad is no good
Cause later they will not forget.

The Biggest Bully

Some of the biggest bullies in history
Have always been taken down
They fail to align with a Christian sign
When wrong comes tumbling down

Let's look at Goliath the philistine
He was taken down by a rock
One that David picked up off the ground
And used it in Gods a Slingshot

Then let's look at the pharaoh each
Who didn't let a people go
When given time after the signs
God's newest fan was a pharaoh

Then you have slavery in America
A people that shall and did overcome
Life was lost but was the cost
Emancipated, look what we've become

Now a man boast where he stands
And throws his weight around
A man with a wig whose actions are big
Will soon come crumbling down

Terrioristic Motives

People aften look for motives
Behind everything
They just can't except the fact
A thing is just a thing

Whether someone breaks a vow
Infidelity is the reason
Trying to understand "why"
It may just be that season

People tend to leave people
And families tends to suffer
Regardless of their actions
A families life gets rougher

Someone walks into a church.
Or takes out a casino window.
To fire upon a crowd of people
Weirdos are just weirdo's?

People search for a reason.
Or some kind so rationale
For the actions of a human being
Whose results are so surreal?

A terrorist is classified.
As one who frightens others.
Taunting lives of the harmless
Thy sister and thy brother.

Just Another Black Man

Just another black man
Is all I will ever be?
All they see is color.
They will never see me.

They do not see kind.
All they can see is hate.
I try to keep to myself.
But color is never late.

It is the year 2020.
A lot of time has passed.
The movement of civil rights
Still blacks are harassed.

They do not see educated.
They see that uppity nigger.
As if we all deserve.
To be something lesser

They do not see a family man.
A wife and kid's content
A foundation standing on Christ.
A marriage heaven sent.

They do not see a military man.
Fighting for the freedom of all
We are just another black man.
Nigger is what we are called.

Just another black man
Is all they will ever see?
Know that I see you to
And still, I want to be me.

Proud to be BLACK.

Proud black man
Till it is time to go home
Proud black man
A stallion; Thera bread Strong

Proud black man
With two sons to raise
Proud black man
See their papa praise.

Proud black man
Bringing home that bread
Proud black man
Always mean what is said.

Proud black man
Go to work every day.
Proud black man
Not too proud to pray.

Proud black man
Strong is your being.
Proud black man
Fear is not what they are seeing.

Proud black man
Often misunderstood.
Doing what you can
Because you do what you should

Proud black man
Open those closed doors.
Proud black man
This world can be yours

Proud black man
Lift your black queen.
Not to be hidden
But so, she can be seen.

Proud black man
Your kids, your legacy
Proud black man
Proud they should be.

Kool-Aid Fix

Put the Kool-Aid down
And sir back away
There is plenty where it came from
There is more on the way.

A taste that tasted so good
See puckers that filled their cheeks.
A flavor so fruity
The sugar makes it sweet.

Knowing that when you drink
The flavor takes you there.
Grape, fruit punch, and lemonade
We really did not care.

Long as there was plenty of it.
You could bring it on
Kool-Aid was the drink back then.
Now the concept is gone.

Readymade fruit drinks
Served by the pound.
Takes away the fun in making it.
Watching the drink go down.

Kool-Aid brings back memories.
Even the commercials are gone.
Hey Kool-Aid, not yeah!
Now the pitcher's alone

The Pain of Being Black

There is a certain pain.
That comes with being black.
It comes in various degrees.
Depending on where you are at.

Getting pulled over.
For the color of your skin
In the wrong neighborhood
For what you are driving

Women clutch their purse.
When a black man passes by
Switching to the other side of the street
Makes you wonder why.

Then when you see a man.
Black gunned down in the street.
Anger is the pain we feel.
Just buying something to eat

Even when black men comply.
Still we are gunned down.
They must plant the evidence.
When nothing was originally found

It does not have to be us.
But it can easily be you or me.
They do not see an educated man.
Dead is what they want to see.

Nothing takes the place of pain.
When black is all they see
Afraid of how Black men are made.
Is why I am proud to be me?

Inside A Childs Eyes

Have you ever looked?
Into a child's eyes
Inundated to succeed.

Then at that moment
In their lives
Will they ever learn to read?

I have seen that face.
And I can tell you.
It is not a pretty sight.

You hear anger.
And feel the rage.
They know something not right.

Soon mom and dad
Will not see them in class.
It will be on the news at night.

Because they do not know
What the future may hold
Will they ever get it right?

So rather than
Excepting failure
They choose not to try.

If you are anything like me
You can feel, you can see.
Man, moments feel the eye.

What do you do?
When they look at you
Help is written on their face.

Like any good woman or man
You do what you can.
To help that child find his place.

What kind of person are you?
When they do not know what to do
You can tell they do not have a clue.

Their fears will come out.
Via anger their aggression they shout
The inside of eyes anew.

Too Much to Ask

I did not ask for a Hummer.
I just want a way to get around.
I do not want to be lost.
But if so, I want to be found.

I do not want a lot of money.
But I do want my bills paid.
I do care If my sons are not superstars.
If they enjoy what they play.

I do not want my wife to want for anything.
But I want her to have her desires.
I do not want to paint the town every night.
I just want some quiet nights by the fire.

I do not want to be the center of the universe.
But I do want to be loved.
I do not want my son's to be better than everyone.
But I want them to know what they are made of

I do not want a lot out of life.
But I do want to live.
I just want people to see people for people.
And that is what I would give.

Heart of a Fighter

(Viviana Acosta)

When life knocks you down
You get back up again.
Do not get used to the view down there.
You will just be the average woman.

Following your passion and heart
Since you were a little girl
Now you are graduating high school.
Ready to take on the world.

You took a challenge to stay on a team.
It was in your heart to play.
All you needed was an honest chance.
You waited every single day.

You have always had a talent to lead.
But you also knew how to follow.
Watching people play before you.
Was a big pill to swallow?

You stayed in there and never quit.
And for this you have made me proud
Sharing tears, you will never know.
Behind the smile's tears cried out loud

You have achieved the goal.
Character is built from our pain.
When others hear your passionate journey
Inspired as well, they will remain.

College is your next challenge.
The steppingstone to adult hood
You made it through middle and high school.
College is looking good.

I have coached many players over the years.
Daunted by the things I would see.
So, on this day, the 31st of May
I am proud to say" Viviana Played for me."

Black in America

There is a pain of being black.
Still that pride prevails.
Even though we want peace.
Somehow, we still catch hell.

Go to work and enjoy life!
Is it too much to ask?
Its hard to see it coming.
The smiles are their mask.

Over charge for simple things
Upset when it is met.
How can you constantly take?
And still get upset.

Blessed with the will to survive.
No matter what the occasion
Serving the countries Armed Forces
Not supported by the nation

They do not understand.
When we kneel before a song
With every ounce of our being
We know this country is wrong.

Still we go to bed each night.
And wake up every day.
Tell our kids to live their dreams!
With society in the way

Still when the doors are closed.
We kick them open anyway.
Carrying their weight and ours
That is the black person's way.

Chapter 2

Marriage Do Writes

Married and Proud of It

Yes married, and proud of it.
I love my wife to death.
If she is dying and could not breathe.
I would give her my last breath.

I would pick her up and carry her.
If she could not take a step
She is the best wife in the world.
And how secrets are kept.

Her nature is that of civility.
And she is stern when need be.
I will protect her heart every part.
That is how a MANning should be.

She loves hard and she loves deep.
Which is why it is hard to cry?
For in her fears she sheds a tear
I do not want to be that reason why.

She will go to the end of the earth.
To make sure her family and all is fed.
One reason in life why she is my wife.
Because this is the love, she spreads.

Yes, I married and proud of it.
And I would marry this woman again.
Her dad I would ask without a mask.
Can I have your daughter's hand?

The Heart of a Marriage

I married for the potential.
And I married for the heart.
The growth for potential is good.
But the heart is the best part.

When someone does something
What was their intent?
Did they do it for the money?
Or for the sake of a sentiment

Did they do it for the fame?
An attempt to be exalted.
They feel your pain and remains.
In hopes the hurt is halted

They send you flowers at work.
Or a plant for you to consume.
Loving you because of you
In that heart with so much room

The heart struggles with trust
They are there with extended hands.
Amassing the past from the last
They embrace the shadows of man.

When you marry, marry for heart.
Potential, that can be great.
Education and money's fine
Without heart you seal your fate

The Strength of a Man

A man should have a certain strength.
The corner stone of the home
So that when times get too tough.
The family has someone to lean on

He can feel that feebleness.
Before it even arrives
Make the steps when one has wept.
And dry the tears from their eyes.

Strong enough to ask for help.
Because it is not about him
He will bow his head when said.
God help me take care of them.

Only a man knows his weakness.
And where his strength abides
When you look back on his life
Blessings have no place to hide.

A man in his home sits on a throne
Where he should be proud to sit
He knows his wealth appreciates health.
He does not say I, but we did it.

If she weeps his promise keeps
Prayer is what he should do.
Her hand in mine God is divine.
A back strong enough for two

Love in a Woman's Heart

The heart of a woman
Is one easily obtained?
All you must do is care.
And the love becomes insane.

She will do anything for you.
And you do not have to ask.
All you must do is relax.
Sit back and enjoy the tasks.

Let her know how special she is.
Every single day
If you ask the right way
She will do anything you say.

She has a lot of love in her heart.
How much love is up to you?
If you fail to treat her the right way
There are things she will not do.

The love inside a woman's heart
Is from God and heaven sent?
The love she must give inside
Is dependent on time well spent.

So, do not take for granted.
The love inside a woman's heart
Once love is gone, it is gone.
Someone else will embrace that part.

The Wife Queen

It's okay to love your wife
And treat her like a queen
Take her places buy her things
So that she can be seen

Make her feel appreciated
So her inner beauty will glow
Then she won't think she special
At this point she will know

Something about confident women
You can just see her shine.
The way she Carries herself
You can tell she know she's fine.

That's the power of loving a woman
And doing it the right way
She will more than love herself
And every day is a good day

Children will know mommy is loved
Their daughters and their sons
You have the way for a brighter day
Be it cloudy or under the sun.

When a woman feels this way
Imagine how she will treat you
A woman living on top of the world
Will do anything you ask her to do.

Working Marriage

Don't ever let anyone tell you
That marriage isn't work
You punch a clock every-day
For marriage and it's worth.

Breakfast in the morning
Before you leave the house
I love you babe have a nice day
Kissing and hugging your spouse

You have that subtle phone call
While you're on that daily grind
It may not seem like much
But this is a meaningful time

If you don't get excited
At the sound of their voice.
Evaluating your relationship
Did I make the right choice

Then it's time to unwind
And debrief each other's day
Listen to every single detail
Marking references along the way

Doing chores and eating dinner
Settling arguments as they arise
What matters most you brag and boost
Is what's in the heart in the eyes.

This is just the tip of the iceberg
For marriage is so much more
It starts when you lay down at night
To the time you walk out the door.

Today I thought about you.

Today I thought about you.
About how much I miss you.
Today I thought about you.
About how much I love you.

Today I thought about you.
How you laugh and smile.
Today when I thought about you.
Holding you lasts for a while.

Today I thought about you.
Watching over you when you sleep
Today I thought about you.
Wiping your tears when you weep

Today I thought about you.
Thoughts are filled with desire.
Today I thought about you.
Your heart and soul I admire.

Today I thought about you.
Rising before the sun shines
Today I thought about you.
I am blessed that you are mine

Today I thought about you.
Today, tomorrow, and for always
Tomorrow when I think about you.
It would be just like yesterday.

Snooze Control

Early in the morning
When I hear that alarm sound
I find I must wake it up.
From a night of laying it down

Then I look over my lids
At this woman I chose to wed
I am so glad that she said yes.
As she lays here sleep in my bed

When I hit that snooze button
To give me a little more time
Trying my best to hang on longer.
To appreciate this gift of mine

To see her lying there at rest
Not a peep and not a sound
I wonder who is in her dreams?
Is it Earl the Prince she found?

Does her dream have a meaning?
Can I rescue her in time?
Do I slay the Dragon involved?
Or from someone committing a crime

In the end does she feel safe?
Is life filled with happiness and joy?
Does she have that schoolgirl crush?
Experienced by little girls and boys.

Do we walk off into the sun set?
Side by side holding hands.
I wonder if this is in her dream.
That is how my dreams end.

Then when that snooze button
Rings that final sound
I know it is time to wake it up.
From a night of laying it down

That Moment

This is the moment I imagined.
Spending this moment with you
If we ever got a chance to meet
What would I say, what would I do?

A moment filled with excitement.
But I do not want to scare you away.
It is not often you meet a dream.
That just does not happen every day.

When I look into her eyes
Will I see her heart and soul?
Someone to spend my life with
And love her until she is old.

I wonder if she thought of me.
In the same thought and mind
Probably not since she has seen me.
But it was not the place and time.

I have only seen her picture.
Embracing the thought of her from sight
I would love to hear her voice.
Does it sound like the way she writes?

What would it be like to hold her?
Touch her face, smell her kiss.
See her laugh and embrace our lives.
Is it something that she missed?

Taking time to embrace this moment.
What will this grow to be?
Will it be a fairytale love?
Until the next poem,
we shall wait and see.

The Other Side of Marriage

Every day is no bed of roses.
Sometimes the sun does not shine.
But either way night or day
This woman I married is mine

I amazed she has those days.
When my nerve is at its end
To call her name just the same
I would do it all over again

She must have the last word.
And at times I guess so do I
Two ways to do some things.
And at times we give both a try

When it is her way, she smiles.
So why not let everything be
Then when it is my turn to shine.
It is just not the same for me.

We have words some you have heard.
Others we make up as we go.
Most times we bed and what was said.
Leads to ending we love and know.

The ending is an understanding.
Every day the sun will not shine.
Since it will be forever her and me
Our love is worth the extra time.

We stop to pray thanks for the day.
Then head out for our daily bread.
We kiss and say have a safe day.
For we must lay in the bed we made

To sat and discuss this is a must.
For better or worse we said
We do not leave to come back later.
That was not the agreement.
When we wed.

Unfamiliar Presence

The first time we kissed.
To music and we danced
This was a moment captured.
Closed eyes and instant romance

How it felt to hold her.
Then our lips became friends
What a way to begin a relationship
Ours lips were holding hands.

Michael Bolton and Barry White
Kicked off this grand event.
I would have paid for this night.
Money and time well spent.

Then as we laid together.
We wanted to but did not make love.
It is not that we did not try.
Mother Nature knew what we were thinking of

So, there we lay through the night.
Holding each other till dawn
The warmth and passion that we felt.
Were two hearts again reborn?

Something that was missing.
In relationship we could not do
Was found again thank God Amen.
And I thank him each day for you.

The Relationship Monster

Relationships are amazing things
You go in one way to come out another
Life happens along the way
Forcing you to become the other

You have your ups you have your downs
In love is the you that you found
You also find yourself in hurt
Did that love let you down

Then there's the you that Strays away
Another has caught your eye
Instead of strong and moving on
You cause another love to cry

Then one dies before the other
Leaving a stain on the heart
Because the love you took for granted
Has taken the important part

You sit on days that come in waves
Where memories roll in and out
You try to blame the love you shamed
Those quiet memories tend to shout

It is on those days you find a way
To fight back the hurt and tears
The heart won't stand for your demand
The hurt you hurt will hurt for years

It is on a rainy and lonely night
That your memory wins the fight
You try your best to hold it in
That moment of hurt wins again

The Dream of Us

I had this dream 1,000 times.
About how it would be.
The first time I make you mine
Oh, how sweet it would be.

I would play some music.
To set the right kind of mood
Then I would make a toast
To us ladies first not to be rude

The fireplace would be lit.
With the crackling of the wood
The right cold the right hot
Things work the way they should.

Then I would stroke your face
As the senses kick in
Sight, Sound, Smell, Taste, Touch
Now the fun can begin.

First, I touch you in a place.
As you set free a moan
All the reserve and conserve
With a touch is gone

Then I taste your lips
In leu of taste and smell
Came passion and the hugs.
Pleasure is the story to tell.

Then came the moment.
To commemorate the night
All the sparks and fireworks
Seem to work out right.

In the wake of morning
When we rise in grace
Nothing after that night
Will ever take its place.

A Husband's Gratitude

My wife does a lot for me.
And I do not have to ask.
To pick up a towel off the floor
Is just an additional task.

She comes home and cook.
So occasionally I take her out.
I rub her feet sometimes.
It is what appreciation's about

She washes does her own laundry.
And my laundry is mine
If I have an article of hers
I just wash it to save time.

Taking care of the house inside
The exterior is what I do.
With everything a wife does
A wife will make time for you.

Work was not peaches' and cream.
It follows her home sometime.
It is my job to hear her slob.
Her heart is hers and mine

She does not have to love me.
But she chose to anyway.
With the grace of God, it is my job.
To provide and protect every day.

Taking time to speak my mind.
With you every day is a pleasure
We fuss and fight wrong or right.
With gratitude, you are my hidden treasure.

Close to each Other

When were not together?
We are still together.
No matter where we are.
The feeling keeps getting better.

You never have to worry.
Where my heart is with you
Love may not be for others.
But love is what we do.

Complimenting each other's heart
Whether the sky is blue
You brought me breakfast in bed.
When I wanted to do the same for you

When you wonder where I am
Just close your eyes to see.
When you want to talk to me
Just call me and there I will be.

I will be there to protect you.
With a love that respects you
I guess Michael Jackson knew
What people meant to say I do?

We will walk hand in hand.
Two hearts beating as one.
Not our will be done.
But in him God's will be done

Warrior Wife

My wife is a warrior.
In every sense of the word
She called me crying.
Despair is what I heard.

I yelled "I'm on my way."
I am okay, an associate died.
He passed from COVID.
And is why my wife cried.

We discussed his plight.
And the phone call she received.
His wife called with the news.
And together they both grieved

I asked if she wanted to leave.
"No, we are undermanned."
People are out with COVID.
I will stay and do what I can.

God sent me a good one.
She is the example to follow.
It the face of this pandemic
She refused to go.

I am always here for her.
She was there for her crew.
I could not be upset with her.
For that is what leaders do

COVID has touched the lives.
Of at least one person we know.
Life must and will go on.
And that people, is Life's show.

What I Want

Is a woman who loves?
And wants to be in love.
During a day's challenges
They are all you are thinking of

I want to find a woman.
Who has a deep appreciation?
For life and things surrounding her
The gift that's God's creation.

To find a woman who at this point
Is ready for life to start.
Where I can look into her eyes
And see this woman's heart.

To embrace this woman's voice
And feel support that any man needs.
Be there when times are hard.
And when her man succeeds

A woman who will honor herself.
And honor God as well
To share in moments of the day
Where excitement itself will tell

She holds a passion deep within
That is dying to get out.
A soul God placed upon this earth.
That all men will speak about

Then finally if I must say.
She possesses the desire to share.
In her soul she finds peace
Because in her spirit she cares

All these qualities are hidden treasures.
That she will not flaunt
When I find that special woman
This is what I want.

Greatness

It is not often we encounter greatness.
Every single day
You notice it in the things they do.
And the things they say.

Watch how they carry themselves.
See that greatness shine.
It takes a special person to see.
What was before others blind?

It starts off in baby steps.
Their morals and their beliefs
They can see the disappointment coming.
So, they tend to tailor their grief.

People will genially flock to them
Just to catch a word
So, they can go tell others.
And apply to life what was heard.

They do not have to say a word.
Greatness just shines right through.
Never blowing their own horns
Because other people do

I was fortunate to meet such greatness.
On Zoosk what a site to see
I knew that when I saw that smile.
She would be enough fun for me.

I cannot wait to see the greatness.
On the day when it shall come
They will ponder and then wonder.
Where did Sophia come from?

She cannot see what I see.
This woman I love and know.
I found treasure beyond measure.
And I will never let her go.

Love Earl

Happy Birthday 4/5/2013

Girlfriend and Boyfriend

Girlfriend is a baby name.
Traditional in its sense
Meant for someone you love.
All its passion and intense

Others will not know the meaning.
Only we will comprehend.
We will look across the room.
See each other and start to grin.

Girlfriend this, boyfriend that
No matter what we do
Enjoying each other's company
Because that is what friends do.

We will friend each other.
And even love each other.
Pray with each other.
While embracing one another

Girlfriend this, boyfriend that
Traditional not its intent
Husband and wife
Is what we truly meant?

Wow what a feeling
To have someone like this around
Before we fell in love
Friendship is what we found.

Today I touched an Angel.

Today I touched an angel.
As she began to fall
I reached out to catch her.
To protect her that is all.

This was meeting by chance.
To reach her in the sky
Even though I am grounded.
Today I had a reason to fly.

To see her smile made me smile.
That brightened up my day.
I wish this flight did not have to end.
Where a day would turn into days

I could see us holding hands.
Walking in the park
Listening to some sweet soft music
While slow dancing after dark

Then I would slowly caress her body
While holding her in my arms
Kiss her lips and touch her heart.
To keep her from falling
safe from harm

Thought for the Day.

You will always have a man.
That will do anything for you.
Pay homage to your finesse!
Which is the least that I can do?

Call you on the phone at work.
To see how was is your day.
Letting you know you are loved.
Are words my actions would say.

God made it possible.
For us to share this life
Me as your husband
And you as my wife

As we continue to walk the walk
And dream the same dreams.
We will also talk the talk.
Because devotion is in our gens

We share the same love.
Our hearts are combined.
Laughter is our medicine.
God's word is our lifeline.

This is just a thought I had.
So, I decided to jot it down.
With all the thoughts in my head
This was the thought that I found.

Chapter 3

Parental Do Writes

Grown Little Child

Grown little child.
With her hands on her hips
Little boy with swag
Trying to walk with a dip.

Exposed to grown folk stuff.
Now you think you are grown.
You will find out soon enough.
When living on your own

Talking back to grown folks
Because you have seen some things
It does not make you a scholar.
One day you will know what I mean.

I know the things that happened.
Really was not your fault.
Education will guide you in life.
A smart mouth brings it to a halt.

Some take care of siblings
Some kids run their home.
Just because you cook and clean.
Now you think you are grown.

Just because your boyfriend
Makes you feel a certain way.
Because you think your stuff do not stink
You can say what you want to say.

Be careful what you say and do.
Thinking that you are grown.
Because one day your parents will pass
Then you will have to be grown

Larger Than Life

The Dream

When I was just a kid
my dad was larger than life.
He stood about 10 feet tall.
And carved Turkey with a butter knife

Whenever I was afraid of the dark
He would sit and watch me sleep.
when I woke the next morning
dad was standing there by at feet.

He dueled with the spirits.
And fought monsters all alone.
when dad came out of the closet
The ghost and monsters were gone.

I thought was Superman was then man.
But dad just turned off.
He turned a sore throat and runny nose.
into a mild and gentle cough

I heard a strange noise one night.
And peeped through the bedroom door.
There dad was looking at the ceiling.
With both knees on the floor

I tried to capture his vision.
But walked away shaking my head.
grownups do the strangest things.
so, I just went on back to bed.

little did I know dad was on the floor.
talking to the Lord above
he said this is where he found strength.
where he found peace and love

Dad had some magical words.
That separated the moon and sun.
He said son always do your best.
Live your life and have fun.

Remember always I love you.
because you are my son
and that you have a place to go
when you have no place to run.

A Mother's Protection

I used to think that my mom
Was the meanest mom in the world
She would never let us spend the night
Like other boys and girls

We'd sneak and go outside
When mom wasn't at home
All the kids would get to play
When they were left alone

We couldn't go to parties
If my mom wasn't there
If she didn't know their parents
We couldn't play with them anywhere

Little did I know
There were things my mom knew
People didn't have good intentions
She tried to make sure we had a clue

I look back on those days
And compare those days to now
With all the ugly in this world
Managing to hid it from us somehow

With all the chaos in the world
Mom knew what she knew
Of all the people she protected as from
Was she protecting us from you

Mother's Day

We have rough days.
tough days and enough is enough days.
days you just cannot stand.

We have quite days.
nice days and darling after you days
days you need a gentleman.

We have sighing days.
crying days and oops I am sorry for lying days.
days we must forgive.

We have ouch days, hut days
and mommy I cut my finger days.
days made possible to live.

We have good days.
bad days and you made me laugh days.
days of destiny and fate

We have walk days.
let us talk days and days I love you for always.
days we commemorate.

We have I need you days.
baby let us relax days and movie rental days.
time taken for me and you.

We have wine days.
dining days and let us dance after dinner days.
days I will do anything for you.

We even have etc., etc., …. Days
one thing seems apparent.
it seems like every day is Mother's Day.

Rain on a Sunny Day

I remember when my mom died.
It was like it was yesterday.
The sun would shine like it was mine
Still it rained that day.

I was working writing programs.
When that phone call arrived
My brother said with a heavy heart.
Momma is no longer alive.

My brother being who he is.
I thought it was a joke.
A clearing throat before he spoke.
Is when his voice broke.

I spoke to my sister there as well.
Confirming what he said
I held the phone while all alone.
Man, my mother is dead.

I slowly rose feet and toes.
And went to tell my boss.
I need to leave my mom just died.
She gasped; I am sorry for your loss.

I do not remember getting to my car.
All I remember was the drive.
From MHMR to Parkland and I-30
For most of the trip I cried

That is the day that it rained.
Even though sun was out.
My mind replayed the memories.
I did everything but shout.

At times it was hard to see
The rain would cloud the pain.
I was able to see but just barely.
I could see my mother's pain.

I went to where her body laid.
And it looked like she was asleep.
Her body was cold her body told.
Again, my eyes would weep.

It was hard to except the fact.
That my mom was really gone
Even with everyone around
Suddenly I felt so all alone.

I drove to my mother's house.
Where we grew up as kids
Then the rain started to pour
Remembering things, we did

Playing ball in the back yard
With kids from down the street
Racing under the streetlights
With no shoes on our feet

All the cookouts and Bar B Q's
With church family and friends
Wishing I could bring her back.
This is a message God would send.

It was time for me to step up.
And become the man she raised.
Now I understand as a man.
Why God is worthy of his praise.

I could not be mad, but I was sad.
When God plucked his flower
We should learn when it is our turn.
It can be any day any time any hour.

Dedicated to
Alice Faye Carter Manning Raye

Tears of the 324th

I have never seen so many tears.
Found in one place.
All you could see from wall to wall.
Were tracks on people's face?

This would be a place.
Where hearts could compare
To see if emotions are the same.
On this floor and everywhere

I never thought I would end up here.
Never in a thousand years
Divorcing a woman, I swore to love.
In front of God, fighting back tears.

I know this is for the best.
But it sure does not seem that way.
I cannot wait for the love to stop.
I pray to God for that day.

I guess everyone feels that way.
At least from the teary-eyed aspect
How did a marriage loose so much?
The love, the laughter, the respect

I did not like who I was.
And my son's later let me know.
Even though I love them much.
To them it just did not show

For once I can now admit
That this was a time in my life
I did not like the man I became.
When I called that woman my wife.

Now I am in a better place.
Because of God and his amazing grace
Now when I see my son's.
There is always a smile on my face.

The Game that Never-Ends

The ongoing basketball games.
Never seems to end.
Since I cannot remember the score
We just start all over again.

My son and I are referee's.
Playing one on one between games
Talking noise and making moves
No shot is ever the same.

He scores and I score.
Whooping it up on the floor
A bond my son and I share.
Playing ball like never

When he was a little boy
I had sometimes let him win.
Then I would have to let him loose
To grow and be strong in the end

Now that he is becoming a man.
He is still making me proud.
He would shoot a jumper and drive to the hole.
Then fall while yelling out, "foul!"

I cannot wait to see his son.
And what he will grow to be
Because every day I see my son
He is what I see in me.

This basketball game goes on and on
And never seems to end.
A game I am proud to play with Jasper.
Jaelen is next, he must work to win.

Mack Earl Tippens

My dad is a proud man.
Just turned 80 years old
Refuses to change his lifestyle.
Taking care of his household

Drinking and smoking cigs
Living a life of the bold
Taking care of his wife
Because that is what he was told

Mom attends dialysis.
At least three times a week
Dad makes sure he is her ride.
A vow he continues to keep.

To love honor and obey
To have and to hold
Through ups and downs still around
The marriage thing, I am sold.

I used to call him Mack.
Because that is what I know him by
Now I call him Cat Daddy.
He has 9 lives I wonder why.

Living with most of his faculties
The hearing is somewhat dim.
Dominoes is his middle name.
If you know me, you know him.

He had a certain kind of swag.
You can see it in his walk.
He had a drawl to tell it all.
You could hear it in his talk.

Talking noise and taking names
Most of the times he would win.
I cherish those times they were mine
I would do it all over again

Do not let someone else count your money.
Then just walk away.
A concept that he lived by
And still does to this day.

Mack Earl Tippens is his name.
My dad at 80 years old
A man who lives his life his way
A story worthy to be told.

Grow Up Young Man

I watched my young men grow up.
Ever since they were kids.
I watched them and their activities.
With all the special things they did.

I watched them give speeches.
During Christmas and Easter plays
Watched them play sports.
Yes, those were the days.

I can remember Jasper.
The Brazos League was around.
He intercepted a pass.
And ran it back 60 yards for a touchdown.

I watched him make the difference.
In whether his team would win
He stopped a full back at the 2-yard line.
As he hit him low and dug in

Then there were the fun times
When visits to the hospital was made
Jaelen swallowed a quarter in practice.
Bubble gum anesthesia his medical aid

Then they graduated from high school
Now they live what they have learned.
I told them from a young age.
In life you will get what you shall earn

Life will never take the time.
For you to trial and error for clues
Take the time to educate the mind.
Live life and do not let it live you.

The Proud Parent

Children can change the lives.
Of those they are raised around
Change lives for the better
And sometimes let you down.

What is their motivation?
Or what do they make you do?
Whatever the result of their lives
It always starts with you.

Just by their presence of being born.
They can make you stop the drinking.
Make you put down that cigarette.
Who knows what you were thinking?

Children will steal your heart.
Because that is what children do
Make you stay in a marriage.
Longer than you are supposed to.

Then as they grow and become of age.
They make you say bad words.
You ask them to tell you the truth.
What they did is not what you heard.

Then children can make you proud
Head held high and your chest stuck out.
Make you hang reports on the wall.
That is what pride is all about

When kids grow up to live the life
That you pictured for them to do
They do not smoke; they do not drink.
Because it all started with you

Full Time Mom

As a part time mom
You can say it and you can see it.
But as a full time, mom
You must do it and then believe it.

You cannot be a part time mom.
With full time expectations
You can tell a kid what you want.
But all they feel is your reservation.

Time in, and time out
Really comes into play.
How much time do you spend with your child?
During a day

Is most of the time filled with homework?
Dinner then off to bed
Quality time is mind to mind.
So that the heart and spirit is fed

Kids cannot see or feel the things you do.
When they only hear the things, you say.
Your heart may be in the right place.
But your actions must feel that way.

You cannot just be a hang around mom.
And expect children to figure it out.
It is like when you want a man to be a dad.
But that is not what this poem is about.

In our society today and time
Actions speak louder than words.
SHOW THEM what you want from them.
So, they can hear what they heard.

The Critical Leader

God gave me a message.
To give to my son
It is about a boy leader.
Who can possibly be the one?

People are going to criticize you.
Especially when you fall.
They like you or they do not.
They will curse you all in all.

Leaders are never tripped from the front.
It is by the follower from behind.
Because they cannot do what you do
So, its fault in you they find.

You will often carry a load.
That they cannot even pick up
Something special God gave you.
That in others will never show up

You love the praise when it comes.
Criticism comes along with fail.
You will find you will succeed more often.
Then you will fail to prevail

So as a leader let them talk.
Because they always will
Lead them when they cannot follow.
Soon they will honor your skill.

Followers notice when you lead.
And notice how you fall.
So, when you fall, fall with pride.
When you get up
It is noticed by all.

I Love You
Jaelen Earl Manning

Christmas 2020

My son joined the U.S. Army.
And was granted block leave.
This is a special occasion.
Giving my mind and heart relieve

I know he is in harm's way.
But he has a praying dad.
As he defends this country
Things will not get too bad.

I have reservations at times.
As he defends the civil liberties of all
He will answer every single time.
His country and duty call

He came home for Christmas.
So, he would not have to stay.
And spend his holiday alone.
Christmas 2020 is a special day.

I reflect on all the soldiers.
That have no families to spend.
Who stay on base to plead their case?
Waiting for the holidays to end

Spending that time alone
Eating that Christmas meal
Watching a New Year come in.
The loneliness is surreal.

Waking up in that bunk bed
With no one else around
Except for the other guys
With no family to leave town

The memories and thoughts
That still cloud their minds.
About their family's past
In my hopes were good times

To all the soldiers on base
Who had no families to attend?
I pray that God guides your steps.
That soon holiday loneliness ends

You will finally meet someone.
Bringing loneliness to an end
If I pray and you pray
New holiday memories will begin.

A Manner of Fact

I saw a kid say thank you.
And it really touched my heart.
He had to be about the age 5.
With manners it is a start

He had a little runny nose.
His shirt was buttoned up wrong.
Walking dragging and holding his pants.
Because they were too long

He saw some things he recognized.
And excitement filled his eyes.
It was like he saw it for the first time.
And everything was a surprised.

I told him to stand up straight.
Son, tuck your shirt in
If you want to become a man
Appearance is where it begins.

Take some pride in yourself.
How your walk and how you look.
Your voice maybe raspy at times
So, do not use words not in books.

Wipe your nose little one.
And son pull up your pants.
As a man you will walk alone
Just like the pride of an ant

As Your Father

As your father it is my job
To teach you how to be a man
To teach you that when you fall
You must find a way to stand.

As a man you make mistakes
You must own it like a boss.
Know why the mistake was made?
So, the next time you are not lost.

Help you find your why in life.
Teaching you how to pray.
How you pay homage to God.
And thank him for each day.

Teach you when you find a wife.
She must become your world.
How to protect and preserve her.
And make her feel like your girl.

Teach you all about the world.
And how to make your way
To provide for you family
You must go to work every day.

Then when you have your kids.
You can do the same.
Have a daughter with her curls.
And give your son your name.

Your wife will teach her to be a lady.
As you teach your son to be a man
Then the cycle repeats itself
Now everyone has a place to stand.

Then one day you will say.
Son, you are no longer a kid.
I must teach you how to be a man.
The way that my dad did

The Same

A lot of things in life
Can sometimes be the same.
From wearing the same pair shoes
To having the same name.

The love a father has inside
When he has two sons?
Does he love one more?
Then he does the other one

Does he love them both the same?
As they make their way
Stumbling in life and getting up
That will make them men someday.

Guidance provided for both sons?
Do they need the same advice?
Do you find yourself saying things once?
Or sometimes saying them twice

One stuck a rock in his ear.
The other swallowed a quarter.
Each time I rushed to their side.
Love and patience a tall order

When discipline was applied
One frowned and the other cried
They wished that I would stop.
After things that they had tried

Then there came a point time
When the rod was no longer needed
They took my attitude and temperament.
A character trait deeply seeded.

It is very possible to love both sons.
It does not have to be the same.
And still love them just as much
And value the mention of their name

You love them when they struggle.
And embrace them when they win.
Effort is just as important in a game.
When you lose every now and then

In this thing that we call life
It can be like a basketball game.
Two sons, two different personalities
Same dad, and both are loved the same.
In different ways

Dedicated to my sons.
Jasper Earl Manning II
Jaelen Earl Manning
Christmas 2011

Teach them to know!

When kids want to know
Where to go to find the answer.
Bad info can poison the mind.
Spreading through the body like cancer

Someone must take control.
Be responsible for what they learn.
Teach them how to teach others.
Until it becomes their turn

Kids can be victims of parents.
Inheriting their bad traits
If we do not recognize this travesty
It may be too late.

Not every adult has the knowledge.
It takes to teach a child.
The time it takes to correct the mistakes.
Will take more than a while.

When kids want to know
We should teach them where to go.
This way they can find the answer.
Instead of just saying "I Don't Know."

Will They Hear You

When someone tries to have your back
Then you turn yours.
Try to help you find your way!
But will not walk through the doors.

Try to tell you right from wrong.
But you always chose the latter.
Not caring that we traveled your road.
It was not you, so it did not matter.

Sharing our wisdom and advice
Still the ears were closed.
When it comes to matters of the heart
You will find your way I suppose.

Now you have kids of your own.
Now is your chance to lead.
Will you be able to touch their lives?
Or someone else teaching them to read.

Here is a great piece of advice.
The next time they see you.
Years will mount but will not count.
Because now they cannot hear you

Now it is coming back.
What your parents said to you
Will you children do to you?
What your parents told you not to

Chapter 4

Do Writes as a Man

The Gentleman Thing

There is something special I like to do.
And it is called the gentleman thing.
It is when you are nice to someone special.
Finding reasons to give her a ring.

That age old, honored tradition
Grab her chair and open the door.
Tip your hat when she walks in
Or lay your coat on the floor.

Skim the menu before you order.
To find out what she wants
Order for her so she can relax.
Tell the waiter her dos and don'ts.

Excuse me ma'am may I please.
Have this dance with you.
On one knee the question is asked
Because that is what gentleman do

Then while on this dinner date
Take a sip and toast some wine.
You are thinking to yourself.
That one day she will be mine

Then as the date comes to an end.
You express to her thank you miss.
I really enjoyed this evening.
Then seal the deal with a kiss.

Everything is just about her.
What would she like to do?
This is what a gentleman does.
Anything just for you.

Lifelong Lesson's

Our children are our commitment.
We are all they have got.
They should be able to come to us.
And that should really mean a lot.

From the time they are born
They need our support and guidance.
First, we teach them how to walk.
Then we teach them where to stand

They do not know anything.
Born into this world a sponge.
Absorbing the essence of success
So, their lives will not take a plunge.

Even when their old and grey
They still need our wisdom.
For some reason at any age
Our words give a sense of freedom.

Then when it comes time.
For them to put us away
Our teachings should live on in them.
Day after day after day

Then when they have their kids.
What they learn means a lot
The world will then continue to spin.
With the lessons I never forgot

The Wants and Needs of a Child

When I sit at think about
Our wants and our needs
Are these really items?
That one needs to succeed.

How do they help fulfill?
Our lives everyday
They tend to keep us motivated.
Depending on the need that day

There are many types of needs.
Food, finance, and the physical
We do not need a Mercedes Benz.
But it helps with being social.

A student asked me for a quarter.
She is on free and reduced meal.
All she wanted was some hot Cheetos.
To change the way, she would feel.

This was one of her wants.
 A want that she did not need.
But hopefully when she gets this want.
She will have the need to succeed.

People with money act a certain way.
From people who do not have much
Some had that uppity attitudes.
While to others it does not matter as much

How would she perform in school?
If she did not get her Cheetos
Would she be upset for something she could not get?
Missing answers to questions she knows.

I do not have much money myself.
But I have enough that I can share.
I would rather see her get it right.
Just by knowing somebody cares.

Hopes and Dreams.

(The path)

When that door closes on dreams
Will it open again?
That depends totally on you.
Will it be you, your will or man?

When that door opens for you
Will it shine a light?
Will you pray for what you say?
Every single night.

There are glass doors,
Brass doors, doors made of wood.
Do not be afraid to walk through.
Just remember where you stood.

If you let others dictate
When to open or close the door
You willingly give up the right.
To make decisions any more

You never know what you can achieve.
Until you begin to try
When the door opens, and you walk through.
You will know the reason why.

So, if someone turns the knob.
Make sure that it is you?
Look through doors or knock them down.
Do whatever you need to do.

To a Certain Degree

Just because you graduate college.
Does not mean you know everything.
That piece of paper gives you the chance.
To possibly live out your dreams

Just because your degreed in English
Does not mean you know how to speak.
You cannot talk to everyone the same.
If it is their respect that you seek

Just because your degreed in History
Does not mean you know what happens next.
Even through some things repeat themselves.
Life can still be quite complex.

Then there is that degreed in Math
Where everything must compute
Sometimes the best way to calculate life.
Is to just sit still in mute.

Then there's the Science's
Where you hypothesize each day
The sun may shine on yours and mine
On that bright and stormy day

Then if your degreed, in P.E
You will find life is full of games.
Since it is your dime you must find
The game that will fit your name.

There will be many things in life.
To spark life's fancies and motivations
When you learn to appreciate people
Then you will degree in Special Education

Then what about the Administrators
Who will degree in Mid Management?
Tying together an academic plethora
To what degree was your life spent?

The E in Me

If you could investigate my heart
You would find a gentle spot.
Put there long ago by my mom.
A lady the world forgot.

She taught me how to love.
Loving the way, she did
A life worth living most of the time.
Growing up as a kid

She tried to teach me to be a man.
When there was no man around
I got a divorce after 22 years.
Now, somehow, I feel I let her down.

I always saw what she thought of me.
It would resignate through her eyes
The time she lived she taught me to forgive.
Even on the day she died.

She taught me how to laugh.
With the joy she felt inside
Take care of you family she asked.
On her judgment day I cried

On the outside there is a shell
That people just cannot see through.
If you want to know who this man is
Well that will be up to you.

When I Stand

When I stand
I stand as a black man.
A strong sense of pride
An African American

When I stand
I stand as a Christian man.
Jesus died on the cross.
So, now I can stand.

I stand as a father.
When I stand
Raising two sons
To learn how to stand

I stand as a married man.
When I stand
Committed to one woman.
In me she entrusted her hand

As an educated man
When I stand
I will pass on knowledge.
So, my fellow man can stand.

As a grateful man
I will stand.
Blessed with another day.
All I can say is Amen.

As an Air Force Man
When I stand
I will protect this land.
So, my Grandchildren have a place to stand.

As a righteous man
I will stand.
When no one is watching.

When I stand
I will stand just as a man.
Equal in all its rights
Till there is no color in this land

The Honor in Commitment

The honor of a commitment
Is willing to die for what you believe in
Knowing that if you had to do over.
You would do the same way again.

You give your time and effort.
Only for the cause
Excepting no rewards
And looking for no applause

The commitment that you make.
Will hopefully make things better.
No matter what the obstacles
You follow procedures to the letter.

The commitment that you have
Is to face one greater than you?
Focused are the lives you affect.
Because that is just what you do

There will be casualties.
Somewhere along the way
All you can do learn from them.
So, there will be better days.

The honor in commitment
Is to die one; live all.
For it matters how you stand in life
To find honor in where you fall

Childhood to Manhood

A child picked the flower.
And held it in his hand.
The flower was very pretty.
far from the side of man

He traveled all over the city.
Pretty things came to sight.
He watched the water calm the day.
As bugs lit up the night

He watched the ground wake up.
and the sky bed down at night
he watched the day roll over.
as darkness applauded sunlight

Then as he grew older.
His sights began to change.
Watching people come and go.
While nature stayed the same

As age complemented the mind
He began to understand.
The difference between night and day
That day he became a man.

He picked another flower.
while wiser and much older
the flowers were no longer pretty.
the flowers were now beautiful.

What Do You Expect?

We should demand effort from kids.
Rather than nothing at all
A kid without expectations
Will sooner than later fall

If we set the bar high enough
They will stumble instead of fall.
Then they can help themselves
Instead of you receiving a call.

Our society has come to expect.
Nothing at all from our kids
Why give them anything less
Then what your parents did

If we do not push our kids
They will not have anywhere to go.
All their efforts will be in vain.
With not much in life to show

If they do not have much to show
Then what is their motivation?
If they feel we do not expect much
We will embrace our already nation.

Things must change in society.
If this world is to turn around
They will not have anything to look forward to
If their head is always down.

The Three Hads

Sometimes you can have a good thing.
Starring you right in the face
And fail to appreciate its value.
Wrong time, wrong life, and wrong place

Then at times paths may cross.
Or land right there in your lap
You see it; you feel it too good to be true.
Common sense taking a nap.

Then you have opportunities
To see, want and then take a chance.
You see it, you like it, then buy in
Now for the rest of your life you dance.

Other people's misfortune
Lead to some people's good faith
Soon you have what others cannot have.
Now they will just have to wait.

It is everything you dreamed of
A life filled with never.
Times you can do just nothing at all.
Like they say less is more

Now others can only watch.
Realizing truly, just what they had
You had it, could have had it, and then let it go.
Now it is just too bad.

Finding someone that appreciates
The true essence of what God made.
A lifetime filled with happiness and dreams.
A gift that with love is paid.

The Other Side of Heart's

We all want the side of the heart.
That everyone seems to know
A lifetime of love, happiness, and joy
That is not always how things go.

I have entertained your deepest fears.
I know just how you feel.
Giving your love, your heart and soul
Only to find it was not real.

You give it your all 100 percent,
Loving to be loved in return.
We are both at the same place in life.
Our hearts bruised and burned.

And yet with the help of God
We have managed to persevere.
Hearts will fall, as spirits rise.
Through God's grace we are still here

We have seen the wows, highs and low.
And felt that hurt and pain.
Hoping to find at some point in time.
As for fantasies we want the same.

We have heard it all and seen it all.
So, words do not mean a thing.
Ours actions will dictate our thoughts.
And that is what we should bring.

So, I understand just how you feel.
And the reservations you feel inside.
Of all the people in the world, we met.
And through Christ,
The magic of love will abide.

Afraid to Love.

Do not be afraid to love your wife.
When you do love her loud
Love her your wife so much.
That your love stands out in a crowd

Love her so your children can see.
This is how a couple should exist.
So that when they grow up.
Your kind of love is what they miss.

Now they have a model for love.
And this is what they will seek.
They will not except anything less
A love that is strong not weak.

Let your love be that guide.
Our sons and daughters will rise.
They will have a love so strong.
That you see your love in their eyes

Ladies love your husbands as well.
Not just to hold their hand
Even though he stands upright.
There's confirmation to understand.

Do not try to train him.
Love him for the man you met.
If you try to change him
You end up with the man you did not get.

He will show you who he is.
From love he saw as a kid
That is why were in this together.
Doing what his parents did.

Control

Part of living a healthy life.
Is to know what you can control.
This one simple understanding
Will determine how you grow old.

Let us look at these things.
And understand what control may be.
The sun is going to shine.
No matter how you look at it, you can see.

You cannot control the weather.
But you can control what you wear.
You cannot control what other people think.
And it might be scary inside of there.

You cannot control death.
Because you live and you will die
Since you cannot control Gods thoughts
It is not ours to question why.

So, if they choose to walk away.
Or if they choose to stay
You cannot make someone love you.
And that's life at the end of the day.

They may make comments.
To try and destroy your being.
Put your emotions in your pocket.
One thing they should not be seeing.

So, if they chose to take that walk.
Then let them take that stroll.
Cause when that cloud of emotions clear
You were the one in control.

Father Figure

We all long for a father figure
That at times we express concerns.
Somewhere during the conversation
There is a little something to learn.

It could be anything.
Marriage love, bullies, and bills
It does not really matter at all.
Still you must climb that hill.

Opening the mouth to say a word.
Embracing the wisdom, they speak
Longing for a sense of knowledge
To guide you along a path you seek

Understand that knowledge is tough.
When the culpability falls on you
Understand that wisdom is wisdom.
Personal depends on what you do.

Sometimes a father figure
Can share some bad advice.
Depending on how they live their life.
When asking you should think twice

Were they there during adult hood?
Did they stand by you as a youth?
Even though they mean well.
Their wisdom may not be your truth.

If he tells you to bow your head
And let us pray together.
Deep within he understands Amen.
You both will rise to be better.

Just because they have a child.
It does not make them a man.
If what you hear captures the ear
A father figure is somewhere at hand.

A Man is as a Man Does

A boy has got to see it
Every single day
A man gets up to go to work
Trying to make a way

For his family to live and eat
Surviving day-to-day
Walking with his head held high
While kneeling at night to pray.

Working when its hot outside
And even when it's cold
Working hard as a young man
While he's growing old

Coming home from work at night
His family is his refuge
His pride is a result of his joy
Happiness for his family is huge

A boy has got to see a man
Go to work every single day
To know when he grows up
His family will kneel to pray

Loving a woman, the right way
Loving a man, the right way

Can a man be vulnerable
And still show the strength
A woman needs to hold a seed
And love this man at length

A woman can use a man
Who know how to hold her hand
So when her tears decide to run
Her face knows where to stand.

A man who will let her stand
While she holds her own
But when the ground moves around
She has a shoulder to cry on

A man who is not afraid
To let her strength be shown
The world will know where she goes
This woman there is grown

When she lets her hair down.
No one stands a chance
He hearts her hand when they stand
Empowerment is the romance

This kind of man has a strength.
Any woman would embrace
So that in that fun she will run.
Trying to get caught in the chase.

The Face of Death

How do you look death in the face?
And never turn your head
Knowing in a matter of seconds
Your pronounced dead

We all know it is coming.
But we know not place or time.
Life can just be rolling along.
Gone at the drop of a dime.

Death will not tap your shoulder.
It will not whisper in your ear.
Tell you that your time is up.
Despite the gathering of tears

Still you must wake each day.
If you happen to be on God's list
Take the time to reflect the mind.
Did you live a life to be missed?

Death can be a friend or foe.
The world will never know.
Live life either rich or poor
When it is time, we all must go.

The Road to Life

When you leave the house for life
You must build your own road.
Will the road you choose?
Be strong enough for your load.

There will be rest stops.
In your life along the way
Just so you can power up.
To stay no longer than a day

When you face adversity
A bridge must be built.
Family and friends will show up.
If relationships do not wilt

If you forget to pay the toll
After crossing that bridge
You may not be able to
The bridge is now a ridge.

Now you must deviate.
From the point of start
For somewhere along the way
Your road became too hard.

But this is the road you made.
And not the bed you lay.
That is in another poem.
Another time another day

Make sure you make a road.
Where the toll is already paid
A road you will travel again.
Because of the life you made

Tomorrow "n" Today

Lord watch over the man.
Who has the will to survive?
Too afraid to take advice.
Filled with so much pride.

What will be his outcome?
If he decides to open his eyes
We all feel your history.
And we will feel your cries.

Your back was against the ground.
But got back up again.
Tried to stand on your own two feet.
The system ties your hands.

All company ain't good company.
Plan your life in the know!
When things tend to go south
Those friends were just for show.

You mom did all she could do
To lead with a firm hand
It is challenging to raise 3 children.
One day you will understand.

Look outside those 4 walls.
That surround you in every way.
I pray you found a way to pray.
To see a better tomorrow today.

Chapter 5

Do Writes Just Because

Funny thing the heart

You make my heart smile.
Every day and night
You make my heart smile.
Turning dark to light

You make my heart sing.
Ring-a-ding, ding, ding.
You make my heart sing.
That is the joy you bring.

You make my heart sigh.
I cannot stand to see you cry.
You make my heart sign.
So, I ask the why of why's

My heart feels at ease.
Whenever you are around
My heart feels at ease.
Ups out way the down

You make my heart rest.
Things seem to get done.
You make my heart rest.
Loving you is so much fun.

My heart feels a pride.
That way down deep inside
Is a heart full of pride?
Because you are by my side

You make my heart appreciate.
The little things you do
You make my heart appreciate.
That God sent me you.

Hear to Ear.

If I could sit on your shoulder
And whisper in your ear
You would laugh and be amazed.
By sentiments you would hear

You would stare and shout in awe.
With some of the things I would say
Because I would point out things
That people do not notice every day.

I would tell you that I love you.
In a different language everyday
Spanish, Chinese, and Italian
Then language from around the way

Knowing that you would have to go.
When really, you would want to stay.
Work is a natural part of life.
But love helps us through the day.

I would tell you that your breath stinks.
Or how nice you really smell.
People would wonder why you smile.
If you will not, then I will not tell.

That there is a little man
Sitting on your shoulder at times
When I think of you as quiet as it has kept
You are on these shoulders of mine.

Lay Her Down to Sleep

Lay thy head upon they chest.
Now we both can rest.
By the minute she moves a mile
Now no head no chest

What prevents her lack of rest?
Where her spirit will not keep still
Obviously, there is something wrong.
Is it aligned with Gods will?

Is the household taken care of?
Are the bills being paid?
If they are not, there is not spot.
No matter how the bed is made.

Is her love life truly fulfilled?
A question that should be asked
Does she go along to play a song?
Who is behind that mask?

When she finally settles
Is there a smile on her face?
Is there a nestle to the body.
Where the spoons fall into place?

In her mind she will find
A happy place to retreat.
She will not move in that grove.
Because now she can sleep

Softball with a Soul

Softball season is about to begin.
USA, and high school too
I have got the best seat in the house.
Under skies, God painted blue.

Standing in the field
Embracing the dew after dark
Umpiring a fast pitch softball game
At a local neighborhood park

Parents watch their teams play.
In a game where families have fun
Singing and chanting phrases
While softballer's bat and run

The air fresh and clean
Untainted by cigarette smoke
Hickory smells of grilling grills
After meat is tenderly smoked

Left with a comforting feeling.
Wishing that contentment can last.
Knowing when you wake up tomorrow.
That feeling is now part of the past.

Then to wind down the day
Where innings are beginning to end
The best part of the stimulation
Is that next week we get to play again.

Make it Work

You go to work every day
Check in and punch a clock
Then go home time is gone
To your family you're the rock

Lights go off you turn them on
The bills have to be paid
Constantly working a 40 hour week
Still, not enough money is made

They love you to death for what they get
This family you've come to know
Even when tired you're still admired
And your family continues to grow

You don't know why but somehow
Things tend to work out anyway
You make it work when you go to work
Because and night you kneel to pray

Finding a way to smile through
But you can't let them see you cry
You make it work when nothing works
Because your family is your grows

Your family grows and comes to know
This man they call their dad
Worked every day just to make a way
To have the needs they had.

The Land of Math

(In Plain Sight)

Once Upon a Time
there was a number line
X was his name
and integers what's his game

Negative integers on the left
Positive integers on the right.
X could count forever
All day and all night.

Then his brother came to town
Y was his name
The funny thing about both
Is that they both looked the same

It was hard to tell them apart
When laying side by side
So Y would go vertical
Hum is what math replied

So X would come first
Then would come Y
When these pair were ordered
(X,Y) Math would know why

They needed a new name
When they were seen together
These lines were coordinated
A coordinated plane sounded better

They would invite others over
Their friends where named dot
You had to have (X , Y)
For dot to find a spot

X would always come first
Since he was the oldest
Y would always be second
Because he was the boldest

This is how they coexisted
These brothers ordered pair
Coordinated plane their last name
Math knows they're there

The C in Me

I am often reminded of my youth.
When everyday things occur
Smell, taste, and touch
Brings me to things I prefer.

Like the smell of hickory burning
Down home Bar-B-Q's
Gathering hands and saying grace
That is what grateful families do.

Seeing the look on everyone's face.
That is what I enjoy.
We did not know it but back then.
Laughter was our toy.

Old people racing the young
Skinning up their feet
Upset because the shoes did not work.
The grown-ups would hate to get beat.

After they would finally win
Stories were soon to follow.
Listening to the excitement in their voice
Made the food easier to swallow.

I miss those days way back then.
The laughter and the smiles
Wild roosters and rattlesnakes
Memories that stay for a while

A salami and egg sandwich for breakfast
Took me there today.
I am just a good old country boy.
What else can I say?

The Power of a Song

The power of a song
Can invoke so many feels.
People can tell from your actions.
The specials and the real

Whether you want to love someone
Or hate them to the bone.
A song will just reveal.
What you were feeling all along

A song will expose your spirit.
The right song will pull it out.
How your respond when it is done.
Will reveal what you are all about

A song can bring about tears.
Or spark a joke deep inside
It will find that place of excitement.
And everyone else is along for the ride.

A song can give you a sense of pride.
While others will put you to shame
Life is can be a vicious circle.
Their song made you feel the same.

A song will make you dance.
And it will make you rejoice.
The song that you respond to
Is the sound of your voice.

A song can spark a memory.
Take you to a place and time.
Bringing back someone packed
Songs Confined by power of the mind.

A song can spark so many emotions.
Especially if you care.
If a song can have this type of magic
You should try a prayer.

That Final Feel Good

Ever reach for a happy thought
To be tainted by something nil
When all along all you wanted
Was to feel something that real.

Feel a true sentiment.
Are just to know that someone cared.
Someone you knew needed protecting.
So, you took on their scared.

Every time they spoke a word.
You could feel their pain.
Even when the subject changed.
That pain remained.

You tried to feel the good
But everything felt so wrong.
There has a certain place in you.
An emotional feel still strong.

Then one day after you pray.
The answer sends you an email.
Now feelings have new meaning.
Touching that place of fail.

It feels good to finally let go.
And not have to guard your heart.
Wonder why through all the cry.
This did not happen from the start.

Before you sink you should think
If it was peaches from the beginning
Your relationship with God would suffer.
Now through him you are dreaming.

Then when you get that feeling.
Now you have permission to feel.
This is what has been missing.
A prayer from God is now sealed.

Selfish until Death

The wrong time to die.
Is there ever a good time?
Inconveniencing family and friends
What was on his mind?

Didn't he know I had to work?
I cannot afford to miss a day.
Just inconsiderate as hell
But they had to die anyway.

The rent is past due.
And a car note needs to be made.
But no, they had to die last night.
They could not wait until I got paid.

How am I going to make the funeral?
This is going to be tough.
Then my car is not running right
As if that is not enough.

They died and left all these bills.
And their credit was shot.
Man, it does not make any sense.
Even the funeral cost a lot.

Seven thousand dollars
Just to put someone in the ground
They could not have just dumped the body.
In a place where it could not be found

Sure, their kids played with mine
I saw them occasionally.
They always had an attitude.
I cannot ever remember a smile.

But I will try to make the funeral.
Because it is the right thing to do
I am going to plan when I die.
I would not wish this on you.

I used to be that guy.

This is coming from a guy.
Who used to frown his nose?
So much ben gay was in the gym.
It came through ole school's cloths.

Sitting on benches rubbing it in
Your day will come young blood.
Little did I know way back then.
Their words would create a flood.

This is coming from a guy.
Who never had these worries?
Where there was no pain
Now seems to come in flurries.

My eyes do not see some things.
The way they used to
Now when I look at a woman.
Sometimes there are two.

When someone is speaking
They have to say it again.
Now they give me that look.
That I gave ole school back then

When my wife and I take a stroll
My knees have a mind of their own.
I can feel them leaving me.
Someday I know they will be gone.

I know that I am truly blessed.
And you can see the pain in their eye.
I know what that pain looks like
Because I used to be that guy

People are just People

People are just people
Whenever you pass them by
So what harm can it do
Open your mouth and just say Hi!!

When you bleed they bleed
The blood is still red.
So why is it you find hate
Just see love instead

A smile can be contagious
So why not just smile back
People have a want to laugh
When happiness Is an act

Certain times in America
Change was not embraced
People not seeing as people
All they could see was race

Someone once said
A change is going to come
A change to come for all
A change not just for some

People are just people
We bleed we laugh we cry
We work and we pay taxes
Someday time will pass us by

He Looks Like Me

Growing up black we had heroes.
But that hero did not look like me.
Did not think much of it then.
Just thought it was how it should be.

Superman could leap tall buildings.
And Batman was just plan cool.
With the flash being right on point
I could not wait to get out of school.

Racism has always been there.
Choose to believe it or not.
As years would reveal the tears
Prejudice still held its spot.

Then we got a black president
The dream from King was at hand
Life now had a different view.
More of a reason to stand as a man.

A president leading with style and grace.
With one woman by his side
Barack and Michelle Obama
A strong sense of black marital pride

Then came Chadwick Boseman.
The African king of Wakanda
Blessing the world with Black Panther
Disguised and King TaChala

The poise and dignity in this role
Presented a wisdom we could see.
Proud as can be on my T.V.
Was a hero that looked like me?

Women were strong because they were strong.
And not leu of circumstance
A sense of pride you could feel inside.
Consumed by a personal Alliance.

Men were men because they were men.
Leading their families and wives
They woke up every single day.
With an intention to live their lives

His role would just pave the road.
For what a people who stand can do
A nation full of pride and success
A dignity to be found in me and you.

Now my search is different.
Whenever I turn on my T.V.
Now I look for a hero.
A hero that looks like me.

Success in Failure

A person will not know how to get up.
If they never fall
Some enjoy the view down there.
Instead of standing they crawl.

To be a success in life
You must sometimes fail.
Can you deeply appreciate heaven?
If you never go through hell?

Some must go through experiences.
So, lessons will sink in
Some just must see it happen.
To know where a person's been

Some people must fail.
In order to succeed
The view looks a lot better standing.
Then it does to crawl through weeds

Learn from those who had to struggle.
And make that sacrifice.
Someone who is never worked before.
Cannot give you job advice.

The Best You Have to Give.

They are moments in a person's life.
And you happen to touch someone.
A kind or encouraging word.
The only thing to be said to be done.

To change a person's life
And put them on the right path.
Where years add up to success
Now you do the math.

Taking to the road upon graduation
No money, no car, no plan
Made his way to a university.
Years later, he graduated a man.

Touch someone else's life
As s teacher or a friend
Let them know where life began.
Does not have to be where it ends.

Then when their life changes
And they look to you for thanks.
This is the time when in your mind.
Your words turn into blanks.

You know what they went through.
And you know where they have been.
Before they used to be your student
Now they have become your friend.

Touch someone else's life
And help them be their best.
Let their lives influence others.
Because of them you are blessed.

Inside a Black Man

Where does a black man go?
When there is no road
Where does he lay his hat?
Tired from carrying his load.

Where does he find a peace?
At the end of a day
Where does he look for solace?
When he has lost his way

Where does he find the courage?
To keep moving on
Where does he find the strength?
When he needs to be strong

Where does he find a place?
When he wipes his eyes
Where does he find a shoulder?
When he feels a need to cry

Where does he find the sun?
When cloudy is the day
Where does he find comfort?
When loneliness is the pay

Where does he find God?
And what does he have to say?
Where does this black man?
Find a knee to pray.

Where does he find his heart?
When his soul starts to bleed
Where does he find leadership?
When he is expected to lead.

Where does he find the will?
When everything was taken away
Everything except his pride
Is all he has at the end of the day?

Why does a black man fight?
What reason, what is the drive
Only black men will understand.
He fights because he must survive.

Somnolence

The world will not let him rest.
Always on his heels
Finding fault in all he does
He has not time to heal.

His soul bears the burden.
Of living life while black
There is no tan for this man.
His life is not an act.

Women clutch their purse.
While cops pull their guns
How can he stand strong?
When given the option run

The world will not let him rest.
What does the world fear?
Filled with flamboyance and flare.
But no one will stand and cheer.

The world will not let him rest.
When he lays and closes his eyes
His family is depending on him.
He has no choice but to rise.

Rise up from his quiescent
As he rises to be a man
Building emotional antiquities
His children are proud and stand.

The world will not let him rest.
Weary as times may get.
Never get tired of doing right
This life is not over yet.

RAF Alconbury Spartans

As I look back on the times
And all the fun we had.
I look at how far I have come.
Now a husband and a dad

We all used to hit the streets.
We have all done our dirt.
Still we got up the next day.
And we had to go to work.

Hanging out at the NCO club
All-Nighters and we would dance.
Whisper something in her ear
Enough for an evening of romance

Our friends became our families.
Hanging out with gym rats
Friday night football games
Basketball and baseball bats

We did not know where to go,
Or even how to get there
Traveling around town to town
St Ives was our where.

Everyone was tied to the base.
Alconbury family and friends
Some of my fondest moments
Memories that will never end

Things I Can't unsee

Things appear you can't unsee
No matter what the light
Rights you can't wrong and
Wrongs you can't right.

Like a man shot in the back
The knee on a man's neck
A man hung from a tree
Spit on, total lack of respect

A child who is starving
There is no food on the table
A man who will not work
Even though he is able

A man that will not pray
Even as his world burns
A child who is able to read
What lessons has he learned

Then there comes a light
But not the one in the sky
A light you cannot see
Unless in someone's eyes

A person that lies to your face
The way it made you feel
A hurt that is so unbearable
Pain is what makes it real

Frames with no pictures
Just an empty space
Memories that flood the mind
Feel that empty place

A people who storm a Capital
With a tyrant is their leader
Filled with lies, and insolence.
Yeah, I do not understand it either.

Little Stinker

Stepped into the restroom.
Just to take a leak
The stench was so foul.
It was in my clothes for weeks.

I could tell early on.
That he was the man of the house
This smell was so strong and all along.
He would choke life from a mouse.

Suddenly the toilet rang out.
As the water rushed to the lid
Then out from the stall
Stepped a little 7-year old kid.

Are you going to be okay?
Was the question I asked?
The smell was so bad.
Before COVID I needed a mask

Then he just smiled and sighed
Man, that felt good.
Knee high to a water bucket
Was how tall he stood.

How could something so foul.
Come from something so small.
That was the smell from a man.
200 pounds 6'6 inches tall

Then as he left the bathroom.
All I could do was shake my head.
I finally came up with one solution.
Something inside of him was dead.

Personal Journey

They are things that happen in life.
That you just must shake your head
You are where you are.
Because God chose you instead

The road you took to get there.
Was a road no one has traveled?
There were times when you could not see.
As your world began to unravel

People help you along the way.
Because God put them there
Then he held you in his arms
When you thought no one else cared.

Your parents told you this.
And your parents told you that.
Still you did what you wanted.
Now you must where that hat.

The road you traveled is your own.
No two trips are the same.
But we all reach a point in life.
That through the power the glory Amen.

So, when you see others in a place.
And you wonder how they arrived.
Not knowing where they have been.
They may just be lucky to be alive.

The Wrong Team

I can remember watching Cowboys and Indians.
Where the cowboy rides away
Up early in the morning to watch.
Cartoons and westerns on Saturday

Cheering for the white man
Thinking the Indians were savage creatures.
But when I look back now
They were protecting their land and its features.

Not knowing where they white man came from
They just showed up one day.
Now they must leave their lands.
There was a Trail of Tears needless to say.

Fast forward hundreds of years later
It appears we were cheering for the wrong team.
This was supposed to be the land of opportunity.
But what about Native American dreams

All they wanted was to protect their homes.
And persevere their way of life.
The European settlers took that away.
By killing their kids and wife

Now its hard to watch a western
Knowing what I know now.
All I can see is the pain in me.
Some native Americans survived somehow.

They wiped out entire tribes.
And took away their land.
"This land is your land; this land is my land."
Total disregard for the color of man

The pain of the United States
Runs deeper than ever displayed.
Now that America has been awaken.
Lies fulfilled with promises never made.

Chapter 6

Christian Do Writes

SUCCESS!

No one is more surprised than he who expected less.

A Prayer for the Living

Lord God Almighty
Who watches from above?
Thank you for your son.
Who died because of love?

Thank you for waking us.
To see a brand-new day
You watched over us at night.
And sent us on our way.

Touch the hearts and mind.
Of the evil and the wicked
So, they may know your love.
And sway from their convicted

Watch over the little children.
As you call them home
Victims of parental choices
Sitting by you on the throne

You have touched the blind.
So that they may see
Touch the ones who have sight.
So, they may find thee.

Help us embrace the ten commandments.
They have been here at our palms.
Strengthen the marriage of many.
As we reread the book of Psalms

We really do not deserve your love.
But you love us anyway.
At times I know you shake your head
Therefore, we pray.

A Creation Gone Bad

I wonder how Jesus feels
Watching his creation In disarray
This is not what he had in mind
When he rested on the 7th day

The children are being disobedient
The parents have no say
While others stand around looking
Thinking everything is OK

Everyone has a gun
The law is out of control
Is this why the floods came
Is it what the Bible foretold

Men will become lovers of themselves
And the women will to
Forcing others to succumb
To the evil that they do

Leaders will go, leaders are call
Then some leaders just went
You can tell from their actions
The leaders who were not sent

With this new media technology
The world has a firsthand seat
The floods were God's appetizers
What will he serve as the meat

Still we have yet to see his ring.
As the story was once told
The sun will pass, there will be no cast.
The heat will be a permanent cold.

Just the facts

It is often said.
Evidence can incriminate.
What about miracles
The problems they create.

Stories of blind men
All of whom now can see.
Gossip about men of mute
now sing sweet praises of thee

Disciples who arose in fear
Woke a man from his sleep.
It is said he restored their faith.
When water with him found peace

He made a friend rise and walk.
Who died as life passed?
People looked in disbelief.
How? is all they ask.

A man in question asked.
what is going on?
who is this man of miracles?
who has already left or gone?

I hear of his healings.
People talk about his teaching.
when you arrive in different towns
all you see are his blessings.

a man possessed by demons.
his burdens were lifted as well.
this was the stories and gossip.
that common people tell

This cannot be a normal man.
who heals without a magic rod?
these were no cheap magicians' trick.
They were the miracles of a God.

The Days God Made

People enjoy the simple things.
To make our lives worth while
Like greeting someone they enjoy
That brings about a smile.

They wake up in the morning.
Thank God for being awake.
For watching over them at night
For if they die their soul to take

Breakfast in the morning
Nothing fancy bacon and eggs
Topped with a side of grits.
And toast to make any man beg.

Then off to work they go
Just to make ends meet
Cutting corners meeting deadlines
To make their day complete

Then it is time to call it a day
And make their way to the house.
A home cooked meal what a deal
Time to spend with the spouse.

Soft and pleasant conversation
To find out how the day went
To relax and unwind what a time.
Embracing how the day was spent.

Pop some corn, Grab the remote
And together watch T.V
Taking this time to just unwind
This is the place to be.

With someone you love
Constantly think of this is what we do.
Enjoy the days that God made.
This God's for you

I Spent the Day with God

This morning when I woke up.
The sun put a smile on my face.
All that remained for me.
Are memories of a day embraced

A raindrop landed on my head.
And my whole expression changed.
My cloths remained dry.
And I thought to myself, strange.

I grabbed my coat and head gear.
And the wind took that hat.
It blew off balance slightly.
Yes, strong enough to do that.

That night there was a cold chill.
And I pulled the covers over my head.
I felt kind of funny at times.
It was as if someone else was in my bed.

I asked my mother what happened.
And she said, "son God is his name."
He woke you up with a smile.
And cleansed your mind with his rain.

He picked you up with his hand.
And blew dried your soul.
Then he kissed you head good night
With a breeze you mistook for cold

Son you spent the day with God.
And shared many special things.
That is why minds are laid to rest.
And why hearts are made to sing.

The Luxury of Obedience

People do what they do now.
Taking for granted God's grace.
Sin is almost a way of life.
Making commandments a disgrace

When we grossly disrespect God
And fail to respect his strength.
We will all experience his anger.
One to be concluded at length.

Obedience should be a given.
With his commandments in place
Some people call it Mother Nature.
It is God's anger that is in their face.

He has not done there is more to come.
We will see in our final days.
His anger is apparent.
As we sin in so many ways

His anger continues to grow.
With the passing of each season.
People do not see a need to change.
Because they have no reason

If you object to the grace of God
Go to church and file your grievance.
We should do as he commands us to do.
With having the luxury of OBEDIENCE.

God is Good

God has given man the choice
to choose right from wrong
Depending on choices made
Days can be short or long

The short days things go right
Everything falls into place
But when you have those long days
Every minute shows on your face

Let's look at some of those choices
And then examine your day
Are you that Christian to trust in God
To help you find your way

Do you hate when you can't relate
Passing your judgments along
Telling others how they should feel
Yeah, that's not right it's wrong

Did you make a commitment to God
To love honor have and hold
In the end when you say amen
Can you say the truth was told

Have you taken what isn't yours
And tried to make it your own
It's called stealing, although appealing
Right is right and wrong is wrong

Trying to rationalize wrong choices
Never does anyone any good
Choose what's right with no one is site
And you will see why God is Good.

That Question

I had a student in the 6th grade.
She touched my heart one day.
She asked me a powerful question.
I struggled to find words to say.

To protect the student's identity
I cannot call her name.
She almost brought my eyes to tears.
But that day it did not rain

She asked me a question.
I was not ready to answer but did.
Why doesn't God like me?
As she dazed upon the other kids

It took me a moment to answer.
But the words finally came.
God is wanting to make you stronger.
His glory will be proclaimed.

He will not take us through things.
Without having a plan in place
He likely used you to remove them.
From another time and place

She appeared to be a happy child.
But she did have her days.
Family members took her innocence.
She tried to enjoy life anyway.

That question caught me by surprise.
Provoking grateful thoughts
Our mom protected us from the world.
A price not easily bought.

I think about this student.
She comes up every now and then.
I always pray that every day.
That she is still in God's hands

Listening to God

First you must learn to listen.
Then learn to obey.
Not everyone God speaks to
Will hear what he has to say.

It comes in little sodalities.
When things are not available
It means it was not meant to be.
Until God says you are able

Then things seem to happen
For no good reason at all
For some reason you can Stand
When everything said you should fall

God will send a cock roach.
To make you change your path.
Make you fear a distraction.
You are spared the pain of a rath.

Then God will come in a dream
In a clear state of mind
Everything is laid out perfectly.
Events will be that remind.

Once you learn to listen
You can hear what is heard.
God speaks to others as well.
In can be as simple as a word

The Proud Christian

Every now and then a man
Might tear up inside
Elated by his accomplishments
Filled with so much pride

The house finally payed off
The kids graduated from school
Dad got that promotion at work
Man that is so cool.

He's proud of his love for Christ
That he found as a kid
Thanking God when pray
For the things he'll do and did.

When he takes a knee to pray
For himself and others around k
Filled with passion and gratitude
The tears come rolling down.

Then at night when he reflects
About the blessings through the day
He bows his head to take a knee
Because this is why we pray

Wanting and Waiting

God puts us in wait.
Till we see what he wants us to see.
People tell you who they are.
And in life who they will be

He puts us in wait.
Listening for many things
Listening to our hearts
Giving us a reason to sing

We must wait when waiting.
Until God tips his hand
To show us what he has
So that now we understand.

The things in our dreams
Are suddenly made clear.
The want in our hearts
Is the wait that is here?

God has a strange way.
Of giving us what we need
Giving us what we ask for.
So that lives will take heed.

You see the dream on T.V.
Scripts man written for us to believe.
The miracle and magic of love
Is in wait, from God, we receive.

The Day in a Glance

Today I had an opportunity.
To see the day in a glance
I sat down to commemorate it.
Now that I have the chance.

Taking in everything
That God has done for me.
Giving me gift of sight
To see what others cannot see.

Listening to the sound of nature
Because I have ears
Able to embrace emotions.
Because I have the tears

Able to smell natures fragrance.
The hickory and the dew
Then I can steal a sigh
God did this for me and you.

Able to walk and feel the ground.
Because my legs will travel
Able to hold the woman I love.
Because my arms are able

Able to think, what will I do.
When this day should end
Take to the knee since I can see.
Thanking God, I could rise AMEN.

Tears of Angles

A drop of rain
Falls from the skies.
It is what we reap.
When angles cry

Snow is the cereal.
Heaven provides to eat.
It covers the ground.
Our hands and our feet

When it rains
The say it pours.
God washes the wounds.
Of manmade sores

Then the sun comes out
The healing process begins.
Then man screws it up
And we start all over again.

That is why raid drops.
From the eyes of angels fall
It is why they watch on high.
The tears are for us all.

Peaceful Surroundings

Peaceful surroundings can be.
A boat docked on a lake.
Curling up by a fireplace
With a good book is all it takes

Listening to your favorite songs,
With all the lights off in the house
Planning a weekend getaway.
Just you and the spouse

Relaxing in a lawn chair
As birds sing songs of praise
A tall tale by an open fire
Man, those were the days.

Cuddling up to popcorn and a coke
Watching a movie at home
Swimming at night all by yourself
In a pool with nothing on

Walking on a beach at night
Embrace the sea and feel the wind.
For one to enjoy peaceful surroundings
He must first find peace within

The Privilege of Waking up

I did not have to see the list.
Waking up was enough.
There were those who never rose.
They chose to call God's bluff.

There have been a couple of nights
My chest took a beating
God showed his mercy
And woke me with a greeting

Nights when I couldn't breathe
But I pushed out the wind
And God saw it fit
To wake me up again

I know that we're blessed
And why I pray every day
I wouldn't have seen 61 years
If God hadn't made a way

I try not to complain
But sometimes it's a shame
How people go through life
And never speak his name

They woke up all by themselves
That God had no say
Then when they get in trouble
They turn to him and pray

You don't pray after the trouble
You pray before it begins
Giving thanks to God
Who provides support within.

A Passion for Christ

Emotions are a powerful tool.
They control our very being.
When you observe someone laughing
Emotions are what you are seeing.

When something crosses their path
And tears fill the wells of their eyes.
It is because emotions are so strong.
That tears cannot stop the cries.

The love and mercy of a God
Can make you fall on your knees.
Rejoicing saying thank you lord.
Saying, use me any way you please.

They are many things that you can do.
That make you a fool for Christ.
I cannot think of a better reason to pray.
When eternity is the ultimate price

So, if you are going to serve the lord.
Make sure it is with passion when you do?
You may not know what others go through.
But you know what he has done for you.

Well Hidden

Secrets are kept.
Told and discovered.
Riddles are solved.
Because clues are uncovered

The path to eternity
By no means are hidden
Everlasting life
In the good book is written

The secret to happiness
By some are found
Just lift your head up
And embrace your surround.

The secret to happiness
Humbleness is the ride.
Just look in the Bible
It is all right there inside.

He did not have to
But he did anyway

He did not have to
But he did anyway
He put me on a list.
To see another day

He blesses us in every way.
As happiness fills our lives
He blessed us with families.
Kids husbands and wives

He takes a minor miracle.
And corrects a major mistake.
He gives ordinary people a chance.
Who could never catch a break?

He gives us a place to sleep.
And gives us cloths to wear.
Now would a God do that.
If he really did not care

No, he did not have to
But he did anyway
It is why I thank him.
Every single day.

Counting Time

As we look back on our lives
We tend to count the time.
Bringing back the memories
That often flood the mind.

Good times bad times
Count them on one hand.
When the times were bad
That was not the plan.

Then when we count the time.
When things went alright
Those were the times.
Sleep was peaceful at night.

Then you have confusing times
You count every minute.
To find out where confusion began
How you got wrapped up in it.

Then you have the celebration
A time you will not forget.
Every single second
The expectation was met.

Then you have regrets
Times you should have prayed.
Knowing what you know now.
Home, you should have stayed.

Thank you, times, come to mind!
Family wife and kids
Times to smile for a while.
Proud of something you did

In the end you would do it again
Count the times and thrills.
When you think of God's grace
Times when the body chills

Who am I to die?

Who am I to die?
Is there a reason why?
Who can understand?
When my people cry

Before I leave this earth
What did I achieve?
Did I give what God gave?
For the blessings I receive

Did I lend a helping hand?
To my fellow man
Or did I shake is shame?
Not trying to understand

Did mind my own business.
Going about my way
Then Karen called the cops
It is going to be a long day.

Was I treated like a man?
Or even considered as a man
With a knee on my neck
America where do I stand.

Who am I to die?
Did God give me permission?
To leave earth for what it is worth.
Did I finish my mission?

Did I embrace the thought?
Of whom God wants me to be
Did I close my eyes?
And open my mind to see.

Did my family have a chance.
To smile on cloudy days
Did we put the rest any unrest?
In this life that God gave

Who am I to die?
Leaving legacies to sign
Who am I do die?
Was presence worth goodbye?

Giving Thanks to God

After my divorce was final
I spent New Year's Eve by myself
I cried a barrage of emotions.
Until I had no tears left

I tried to close my eyes.
Reruns of life to no end
All I could see was the ugly
Over, and over again

I sent another prayer to God.
This time with a specific request
I just wanted someone to love.
And let God do the rest.

Mom is gone I felt all alone.
I had no one in which to confide.
Previewing my wife my heart my wife
There God was right by my side.

Striped down to the ground
The rebuilding would take place.
I found a church home at IBOC.
So, the pain of past is erased.

Family greeted me at the door.
With a hug gratitude, and smile
Cuz, oversaw security.
As we walked down the isle

Ricky G. Rush is the pastor.
His sermons were right on point.
I could not wait to tell people.
God found a pastor to anoint.

The pain did not hurt on Sundays.
The weeks would disappear.
Inspiring Body of Christ Church
Is how God kept me near

EARLISM'S Part 2

Do not be defined by your circumstance but by your potential. If you do not believe it no one will.

Keep the Press on.

For some loyalty only lasts as long as their influence.

Challenges create change, change comes from awareness.

Nothing shines brighter than new light, and with that light comes new vision.

RACISM! It is easier to dumb yourself down, than to smart yourself up.

So shall ye do, so shall ye be.

Not saying anything says a lot. To not do anything reveals who you are.

People do not follow your demand's; they follow your example.

When you convince someone to have an opinion about something that matters, you control them.

Effort without knowledge is wasted energy especially if nothing is learned.

There are two types of people. Those who ask and those who offer. Those who offer will never ask and those who ask will never offer.

In life and love, positive or negative growth can be painful.

Someone else's best is not your best. Your heart is not their heart. So, do not catch up, WAKE up.

Just because someone can give you advice it does not make it your reality.

Guys be the man you would want your son to be and the man you would want your daughter to marry.

The saddest thing in the world is to have a voice and then loose it.

It is difficult to live your dreams through someone else's expectations.

Let your accomplishments be your bragging rights. NEVER say a word.

At some point give yourself an opportunity to be brilliant.

I find it difficult to explain simplicity to stupidity because the facial expressions never change.

Celebrate diversity, there is nothing like people.

At times silence can be so loud that everyone can hear you.

A person who does not care enough to tell you the truth has no interest in your need to move forward.

When you fall short of your goal, do not get upset get better.

If you happen to be on GOD's list to wake up today, try to be better than you were yesterday.

When you refuse good sound logical advice, you are forced to live your truth. Pain and all.

You build respect from others through self-respect. Be careful of the message you deliver.

Be careful when you entertain ignorance. The seats can be expensive.

When you start living life instead of watching it, the world becomes an especial place.

Running away from the responsibilities of living will only enable the world to control your life.

What you do not say speaks louder than what comes out of your mouth.

Most of the time our environment dictates our circumstances. If you are not strong enough to change your environment, your circumstances will consume you.

It is difficult to dream big when you relish in small thoughts.

The key to happiness is having the understanding that you deserve it.

A leader that needs to be lead is a leader that will be leadless.

You know there is no shortcut to greatness, and why it so feels good when you get there.

When decency and civility become extinct, respect for opinions become obsolete.

How far is your eyesight? Can you see past the tips of your fingers or just to the realm of your wrists?

You can either wake up with GOD or without GOD. Either way life is going to happen.

The book is dedicated to the survivors of the Global
PANDEMIC COVID-19.

AND

In remembrance of those who have
LOST THEIR LIVES AND FAMILIES.

AND

The innocent lives of young BLACK men and women who
have lost their lives at the hands of
RACIST

Index

A

A Creation Gone Bad 105
A Husband's Gratitude 35
A Man is as a Man Does......... 77
A Manner of Fact 57
A Mother's Protection 45
A Passion for Christ............... 118
A Prayer for the Living 104
Afraid to Love. 74
America Is Broken 2
As Your Father....................... 58

B

Behind that Smile..................... 8
Broken Tears........................... 3

C

Chapter #2 20
Chapter #3 42
Chapter #4 61
Chapter #5 81
Chapter #6 103
Chapter 1 1
Childhood to Manhood......... 70
Children with Cancer 5
Christmas 2020 56
Close to each Other 36
Control.................................. 75

D

dedicated............................. 124

E

EARLISM'S Part 2 120

F

Father Figure 76
Full Time Mom...................... 54
Funny thing the heart............. 82

G

Girlfriend and Boyfriend 40
God is Good 110
Greatness 39
Grow Up Young Man 52
Grown Little Child 43

H

He did not have to 119
He Looks Like Me 94
Hear to Ear. 83
Heart of a Fighter 19
Hopes and Dreams. 65

I

I Spent the Day with God 108
I used to be that guy. 92
Inside a Black Man 97
Inside A Childs Eyes 17
Introduction 1, 126

J

Just Another Black Man 13
Just the facts 106

K

Kool-Aid Fix 15

L

Larger Than Life 43
Lay Her Down to Sleep 84
Life's Most Powerful Word 7
Lifelong Lesson's 63
Listening to God 112
Little Stinker 101
Love in a Woman's Heart 24
Loving a woman, the right way 78

M

Mack Earl Tippens 51
Make it Work 86
Married and Proud of It 21
Mother's Day 46

O

Once Upon a Time 9

P

Peaceful Surroundings 116
People are just People 93
Personal Journey 102
Proud to be BLACK 14

R

RAF Alconbury Spartans 99
Rain on a Sunny Day 47

S

Selfish until Death 91
Snooze Control 28
Softball with a Soul 85
Somnolence 98
Success in Failure 95

T

Teach them to know! 60
Tears of Angles 115
Tears of the 324th 49
Terrioristic Motives 12
That Final Feel Good 90
That Moment 29
That Question 111
The Best You Have to Give. ... 96
The Biggest Bully 11
The C in Me 88
The Child Support Files 10
The Critical Leader 55
The Day in a Glance 115
The Days God Made 107
The Dream of Us 34
The E in Me 67
The Face of Death 79
The Game that Never-Ends ... 50
The Gentleman Thing 62
The Heart of a Marriage 22
The Honor in Commitment ... 69
The Land of Math 87
The Luxury of Obedience 109
The Other Side of Heart's 73
The Other Side of Marriage ... 30

The Pain of Being Black 16
The Power of a Song 89
The Privilege of Waking up ... 117
The Proud Christian 113
The Proud Parent 53
The Relationship Monster 32
The Road to Life 80
The Rock 6
The Same 59
The Strength of a Man 23
The Three Had's 72
The Wants and Needs of a Child 64
The Wife Queen 25
Things I Can't unsee 100
Things I Miss 4
To a Certain Degree 66
Today I thought about you. ... 27
Today I touched an Angel. 41
Too Much to Ask 18
Twin Year 2020 2

U

Unfamiliar Presence 31

W

Wanting and Waiting 114
Warrior Wife 37
Well Hidden 118
What Do You Expect? 71
What I Want 38
When I Stand 68
Working Marriage 26

Introduction to the book series

SHOE HEAVEN
"Goldie Goes to Heaven"

Illustrations Late 2022 to follow.